WHEN IN TIME

A Story of Broken Cycles

A'Darianna G. Woullard

CONTENTS

CHAPTER One 1
CHAPTER Two 7
CHAPTER Three 11
CHAPTER Four 17
CHAPTER Five 21
CHAPTER Six 29
CHAPTER Seven 33
CHAPTER Eight 43
CHAPTER Nine 55
CHAPTER Ten 63

CHAPTER
One

I'm zoned out, but awake enough to drive, expertly making my way through the rising evening traffic that's the signature of this city, took me a while to get used to it. As a mother of two girls, both under the age of ten, being able to zone out occasionally is a survival skill. But it's even better when you've mastered the art well enough that they don't notice you're not paying full attention to their endless chatter. I can't, for the life of me fathom how much energy kids can muster. The car is small, stylish, a Mazda 6, the latest version, and it doesn't exactly scream powerhouse single *mother*, as the press release from the University down in Boston I'm supposed to be giving a speech at noon tomorrow, tagged me as. In other words, even though I can manage to tune them out, the size of the car allows patches of the discussion to slip into my subconscious. I can gather that it is about Miss Juliet, my eldest daughter, May's homeroom teacher. Jules, my last born, is playing the supportive sister, adding in her quips and vocabularies that she doesn't fully understand, because she's five and there's no way Jules knows what an hypocrite means. She is repeating May's words back to her. Smart move. Because May is strong willed and a sniff of disagreement doesn't go undetected or un-fixated on. The car could erupt in loud arguments complete with screaming and sulking and general bad energy, with one wrong move. And I'm not in the mood to settle the thousandth dispute.

I grew up with siblings and I don't remember having as much squabbles. But I also acknowledge that we were raised in a different time and were not even close, growing up. The relationship I now have with my older sister, Lorraine, developed when we became adults. Waxed stronger since we now live in the same city. New York was easier to navigate with her help and I'm forever grateful. My brother, Charles stays downtown and also helped as best as he could. We all stay in touch. It's nice having family to fall back on in a new city after literally uprooting your whole life and transplanting into a totally different society.

"Moommm." May's whiny voice reaches me from directly behind the driver's seat.

Shit. The spell is broken, I've been discovered.

"Yes, honey?" I keep my eyes on the road, I have a feeling we might not beat the traffic and if that happens, I'm screwed because asides dropping off the girls at Lorraine's, I also have to make it to the airport before 9pm, for my night flight out to Boston. The two days event, one hour long sit down discussion with the entrepreneurial class at Boston college is something I'm ecstatic about. Juggling several businesses in the beauty industry for years and I finally am getting some recognition. Despite my already busy schedule, I pressed my assistant to include the trip. A perfect opportunity to get a few days off mommy duties.

"You were not listening." I can hear the rising anger in May's voice. I look in the mirror to catch her pulling her mouth in a pout. I sigh as discreetly as I can. The girls love their aunty Lorraine, and she loves them also, Lorraine is unmarried without kids, living her best artiste life, the girls idolize her. Telling them that they have to stay with her for two days made them squeal with delight, but now, on our drive over, May has been acting up. Jules is happy and without worry. She is probably dreaming of all the candies and chocolate chip cookies she can eat under Lorraine's free terrain. But May, there's just something about her energy whenever I have to face my business and leave them with Lorraine. It bothers on spoilt and anxious. I can't explain it. And I also can't blame her, the absence of her dad affects her, probably more than I know.

"Mom?" She presses forward towards my seat, her eyes narrowed.

"Honey, of course I was listening."

"Uh huh." She settles back in her seat with a humph.

"I know you don't like miss Juliet much, but you've to understand she doesn't mean any harm. Telling you to work harder on your maths doesn't make her a witch, honey."

"See! You were not listening!. We finished talking about miss Juliet already."

Uh-oh. I have been caught. I glance at Jules for help, but she just smirks at me. The little criminal. Adorable, but besides the point.

"Oh." I direct my attention back to the road, even though I'm behind a grey jeep that seems to be crawling. I can't blame the driver, the highway is packed now. I dread making the return trip, because by then it'll be much worse. But I'm comforted by the fact that my flight is slated for 9pm. It's 5pm right now. Still got ample time.

"You always do that." May is fully sulking now. Pissed as nails. She gets her temper from me. Jules is all Paul. My ex husband. Pacifist and witty.

"Do what?" I resist the urge to clamp down on my horn in frustration. The Jeep in front of me can really step up its speed.

"Not listen!" May's voice is drawn and high pitched.

Oh boy.

"May, I'm driving. Don't start." I don't mean for my voice to come out annoyed, but it does. May tries to make her seat swallow her by burrowing deep into it like a collapsed doll, looking like I just told her that the world was ending. Fully committed to sulking all through out the journey. I know she'll snap out of it once we get to Lorraine's, but since we won't be seeing each other for two days, I really don't want to part ways on bad terms.

"I'm sorry, but you know driving requires ones full attention, honey. We're almost at Lorraine's, do you really want to be like that?" I turn around to look at her, she has her arms crossed over her chest, seething in her righteous anger, I almost laugh. She really is a mini me. I remember throwing tantrums at the slightest provocation, for the silliest reasons, but my mom definitely did not have as much patience with me as I do with May. One of the many patterns I dedicated my entire self to correcting.

"No." She pushes the single word out of her tight lips. Jules tugs at her folded arms and she smiles at her. My heart warms at their exchange. Motherhood really is a journey ridled with self doubt, fear and uncertainty. Am I doing the right thing? Is this the right way to communicate? Will they grow up responsible? Can I do this thing on my own? What am I even doing?

All these and more, it is even harder when you don't have a good blueprint from your own parents, so you have to work overtime, actively trying to not repeat patterns, not do things the same way, to cut of generational traumas, sever the chain. It is hardwork. But utterly fulfilling as well.

"That's my baby." I give her a smile before returning my

focus to the road. I ease the car into a faster moving lane, cutting off the damn snail like Jeep, the driver is a red haired teenager with a bored expression on his straight face. He looks at me with a frown knitting his bushy brows together, if I was ten years younger than I was, I would have given him the finger.

CHAPTER
Two

I'm back on the road again. It is 8pm, I'm understandably in a hurry. I'm about twenty minutes to the airport, but still I drive like a hound released from Hell. Lorraine had insisted I eat dinner, May, expectedly snapped out of her bad mood as soon as we walked into Lorraine's apartment building. Jules was perfect, a little clingy, weirdly. It's not like this is the first time I'm having to drop them off to go deal with something. But it's never been two whole days.

From dinner, to kissing the girls goodnight in the bedroom Lorraine converted into a mini Barbie getaway theme party for the girls. I was out of the apartment immediately they closed their eyes. Lorraine then started fussing over me, worried about the trip, as this will be my first time going back to Boston since we left. I had to constantly remind her that

I'll be okay, it's just two days, most of which will be spent on campus grounds.

Paul, my now ex husband and I met and fell in love and got married in Boston. We created a whole life together for ourselves there. Boston has a huge part of my heart and will always do. The mutual glue that drew us to each other, had us stuck together for years was mostly shared traumatic history. And that glue wore off when it became clear that he is okay with living life every day as it comes, unwilling to tackle the depth of his issues, unwilling to look deep within and seek solutions. If for nothing, but for the family we were raising. He'd rather seek temporary gratifications. Depressed? Pop a pill. Anxious? Pop a pill. Overwhelmed? Pop a pill.

With motherhood came clarity. I knew I had mental baggages and I was okay with it, so long as it was just me. But with the girls, I realised something needed to change. The momentary lapses in my mental health needed to be checked, properly. Being from a descendant of black people with a tumultuous history of slavery, I know most of the burden are not mine, they are inherited and that made me look insane when I tried explaining it to my therapist who was white. She was kind about it though, but I never went back or tried to talk about it with anyone again.

I wanted to work on myself more, ditch the pills, discover the depth of the trauma, how far back the chain started, why I get these episodes where I'm rendered unable to function properly. Paul didn't. We drifted. The divorce was not dramatic, a smooth simple severance like it never existed, which hurt.

The only issue was the kids, but we managed to find a way around that with amicable co-parenting. It took its toll on the girls, May more than Jules and the only thing that kept me going was the gratification that I was doing it for them. They might not understand now, not that I expect them to, but I'm certain they will come to be grateful for it sometimes in the future.

Thinking of sacrifices, I bit down on my lips softly so I don't crease the lipstick, I had planned to have a discussion with Lorraine about some murky history of the family, from the maternal side. Our mother passed about three years ago from a stroke, then we put my dad in a care home. Lorraine is seven years older than me, she definitely has more information that I am not privy to. This journey of self discovery and reenactment requires some difficult discussions. Probably uncomfortable and might be unproductive, because as blacks, we give less attention to matters of the brain misfirings. I know Lorraine is also on antidepressants, I know she has her own episodes, she chalks it up to being an artiste and the toll it takes being creative as a job, but we all know even if we don't verbalise it. Charles, my immediate older sibling, disappears occasionally. He claims to be consumed by work, but I can guess the real reasons behind his disappearances. We don't talk about it. We see each other when we can and everything else is swept under the rug.

I make a mental note to tackle it once and for all, however uncomfortable, after this speaking engagement is done with. Once I get back. My phone rings, the vibration cuts through the fog my mind has slipped into and I jerked sharply. Keeping my eyes on the road, I swipe around for the phone, my fingers graze it behind my feet, it has stopped vibrating. I take my eyes off the road for a split second to look at the caller's ID, it is Rapheal, my new community centre's manager. I swallow a hiss as I tap to call him back. Raphael has a habit of calling at annoying moments, he always has inquiries to make, questions to ask, it is all good, but I employed a manager so I didn't have to be all hands on deck at every hour. The community centre is still taking shape, but the feedback has been amazing so far. It is my one new project I'm excited about.

I look up to the road and see a car charging at me, obviously out of control, maybe a brake issue or something, I don't have the luxury of mind to contemplate my next action, I swerve to the left, the Jeep zips past me with a sharp metallic scratching sound, and I start skidding out of control. The last thing I think of, weirdly as I give up control over the car, is of my mother screaming at my father on one of those their fights that was a trademark of the atypical marriage they had going on. She was calling him a motherfucker and he was swaying, drunk off his rockers, warning her to stop or he'll hit her. She doesn't stop.

CHAPTER
Three

I wake up to the intense sensation of being surrounded by light. Soft light, not the brash highway lights I would expect. And it is eerily quiet. I am still strapped to my seatbelt, thankfully and my head is pounding. My mouth is dry, and my stomach feels suspiciously empty. The car looks fine from the inside, I feel a trickle down my nostrils, bringing a finger to it, my eyes widen in horror at the blood. That's when I realised what had happened. I just had an accident. My heart drops.

"Hello." A voice I can only describe as stirring, says gently.

If I was not strapped down and aching not only in my head, but every inch of my body, I would have jumped at the unexpected intrusion. I understand that the car is stuck on the levee off the highway and I have been able to sense that a little crowd is gathered outside, some making calls and others scrambling about. I want to turn my head to the sound of the voice, but my neck muscles would not cooperate with my brain.

"I'm Glenda."

The voice says again and just the sound of it fills up my aching head like helium and makes me feel unhinged from reality. Everything outside fades off. Every noise, sound, frantic back and forths, the hovering around the car. Quiet. Am I dead?

"No, you're not, Anna." The voice says again and that is all the motivation I need to finally turn my neck around so I can get a glimpse of the owner of the voice. I'm not mentally prepared for what I see.

It looks like a woman, but by all indications doesn't seem like a typical one. She has short golden locks framing her heart shaped face that looks to be radiating pure soft light. It looks to me, that she is the source of the soft light illuminating not just the car, but me also. I feel like I'm being watched, from the inside out and her light is permeating every crevice of my being.

Her eyes meet mine and I have to shut my eyes tightly, her presence in the car feels both surreal and impossible. Maybe I hit my head too hard on the steering wheel, maybe I'm hallucinating, maybe something has gone terribly wrong and I'm losing my mind. I open my eyes again, slowly, peeking and there she still is. Looking at me calmly, relaxed and unbothered whilst I sit there losing my mind.

"Glenda?" My parched voice feels like torture coming out of my mouth. My dry throat makes the question sound like a squeak. I almost do not recognise it. The car is quiet, too quiet, no sound from the outside. It's like being locked in a vacuum. I can't wrap my head around what is supposed to be going on.

"Yes. I know you might be feeling overwhelmed right now."

Overwhelmed? I'm beyond scared out of my senses right now. Any potential physical injury from the accident is the last of my concerns right now, I'm worried I might have injured my head badly because this just can't be happening.

"What are you? How did you get in here? What's going on?" Each word out of my mouth hurts my dry throat further. It's like pricking my throat with a cacti.

"I am an angel and I have been assigned to help you with your task."

"What task?" My eyebrows knit together in confusion.

"You're the chosen curse breaker. Others have had this task, but you were chosen specifically because you asked for it. For your girls."

At the mention of my girls, I get alert. Things make a little sense now, the knot is unpooling in the dark recess of my mind, gradually, slowly. This is an unbelievable turn of events.

"Here, hold my hand. I can see you have doubts. We don't have much time before the time portal closes."

I hold out my hand, incredulous as I'm sure I'm definitely going crazy, Glenda reaches for my wrist and immediately our skin make contact, I feel a rush of relief. A surge of sweet comfort chasing off every single ache and hurt my body was subjected to from the impact of the accident. I feel like electricity is coursing through every muscle, and repairing them as it sizzles past every fibre of my being. I can't describe, neither can I explain it, but I feel like the contact just healed every altercation I sustained from the accident. We are still in the vacuumed like car, which feels like time and matter outside of it ceased existing, but I'm no longer scared. No longer sceptical. I don't know what this means, but it feels like exactly what I've been asking for. I decide to trust this otherworldly being in the form of an ethereally beautiful woman, her glistening skin that seems to emit light and infuse it into everything she touches, her huge clear eyes, her voice and her trusting presence. I decide to let go and trust instead as wonderful relief surge over my entire being. My body feels better than what I am used to, even before this freak accident. It is like I never was in pain just a few moments ago. I look up to see Glenda smiling down at me, a look of content and pure grace on her face as she clamps down on my wrist and I stare, dumbfounded as my body levitates off the seat, out of the car, and into the sky where an orbiting whirl of energy has opened, swirling particles that can't be felt, a hot kind of heat eminating from within it, I spare a glance back down at the scene below, surrounding my car, an ambulance has pulled up, and before I can make out who is being pulled out of my car, I get sucked into the portal.

CHAPTER Four

THE YEAR IS 1870. LOUISIANA.

Glenda told me this immediately I regained consciousness and the last thing I remembered was going through a warping weird space, a portal after my highway accident. I was going to start hyperventilating, consumed by the surrealness of my reality when she touched my forearm and every anxiety washed off before I could even feel them.

Time traveling? Never in my wildest dreams would I have come up with this.

"So, what are we doing here?" We are in a secluded green field that stretches far beyond what my eyes can see. It is just a vast green space. No human in sight. Pictures depicts classics as black and white, but it has never occurred to me that the reality was not actually in black and white. There is colour and it is lush. Like something untainted, yet. I like nature, but standing here, being confronted by this, I feel like I am still in my head, in an imaginative wonderland.

"We are starting from the root. And we'll go from there, into different time zones to stem the important links that are manifesting in your present life and might be transferred to your daughters."

"Hm, okay. But uhm, where exactly are we? Can we be seen? Because I doubt I'm going to fit in looking as I do. And I have zero intentions of going back in time only to get captured and be made a slave." I look down at my clothes, I'm still in my airport fit that comprises of sneakers, grey joggers and my baseball hat that surprisingly didn't leave my head after that accident.

I have never been to Louisiana, I knew we had history and most of our early family members originated from here, but somehow the place was a sort of taboo for my parents, my mom especially, who got her apathy for the place from her own parents. It just never occurred to me that this long chain of trauma will date back to Louisiana, but it makes perfect sense.

"No, we can't be seen. Which is good because we can't time travel and cause a stir in the time- space fabric. The easier we can sneak in and out, with minimal changes, the better for everyone. I mean, the whole world."

I swallow audibly as her words sink in. But then a question pops up in my head.

"Minimal changes? Come to think of it, you've not really told me what exactly I'm to do."

"Healing. Your task is to help your ancestors heal from traumas they instead bottled up and allowed accumulate over the years through generations."

"Woah. And how do you propose I do that? You're the one with the magical healing powers." I know that might sound saucy, but everything is becoming too much for me. I know I was seeking for solutions, help, anything, so my girls can pass over this curse, but now that I'm confronted with it, standing in a piece of land in the 19th century, the actual idea of it all, I'm tempted to chicken out.

"That is for you to figure out. I'm simply here to help with the time traveling." Glenda says, and her face contorts into what can only be described as a graceful smirk. I don't know what that means, but she is obviously not interested in my whinings. I sound like May to myself.

"And we can't be seen?"

"No."

"And I can't make more than minimal changes else the whole world gets a reset?"

"Yes, in a way."

"Interesting. I would need a minute."

I sit down on the grass. Then unsatisfied, I lay down spread eagle, my brain whirring at a breakneck speed. At the forefront of my thoughts is that I simply can not believe that all this is real. Is someone out there in the universe playing a joke on me? Am I in a coma? Deep in my brain? Is this what being in a vegetative state was like? Weird dreams and shit?

Glenda lies besides me, not touching but close enough that I feel that same weird sensation from earlier in the car, of being lit up from within with the softest golden light. Like soaking up the sunset. I sneak a peek at her, her white dress unstained with the dirt she is obviously lying on and it hits me that all this is actually real. I finally got the answer to what I have needed for a while now. Albeit not what I could have ever imagined, but still, this is my one chance at redemption. For my girls. My whole world.

I make my decision.

CHAPTER
Five

His name is Cents. From his french slave masters, he was the hundredth slave they transported to the plantation, hence the name. His other identity, from before being labelled a slave, erased. A clean slate. He doesn't even know his real name, his real language, his people, his memories starts from the horrible journey here, across the punishing seas, in quite indescribable conditions, but against all odds, he survived and here he is, in a new society, one that judges you based on your colour. One that considers you lesser than a pet, one to be worked to death, one that doesn't even deserve the decency of being looked in the eyes. One to have a permanent downward dent in the neck from never holding their head high.

Cents is a big man, muscular, his skin is an ivory shade of black, so deep, so profound, you could see the sun reflecting off him. It glistens and tells a million stories, all steeped in the horrors nightmares are made of. The scars announce what he was, had been, currently and would forever be, before you even see the man himself.

Cents is my great great great grandfather, according to Glenda and the curse started from him. We are in the day everything went into motion, August 14th, 1870. Six years since slavery was abolished in the state of Louisiana. But of course, that was just for the papers. Slavery still existed, only that it shapeshifted. Into something less morally depraving. Not better, but less in terms of severity.

Glenda directed me to his house, a small shack of a building. In an equally small drab community of black owned houses that bordered more on being shacks, set in a sort of semi circle, on an arid piece of land. Set far, far apart from the residence reserved for the whites. A wide divide, even the air is different from one end to the other.

Cents got his freedom from his slave master five years ago. But that was just a formality, because a free slave has to fend for himself, and the only options were to go back to what they are used to, though this time, it is with a compensation. And the pay was rarely good enough to ensure any actual freedom, so Cents is still stuck, still working sunrise to sunset on the plantation, with his bare hands, rarely a break, his spirit crushed beyond redemption, I fear.

When we made it into his residence, Cents was lying on the carpeted in parts cemented floor, sweat drenched and shaky. A thin black woman is fussing over him. They both have the same mouth, full and slightly curved downwards. I look at Glenda immediately, a confused look on my face.

"His sister. She, unfortunately was raped by a white man. And Cents had him killed in a wild rage. The white mob will be here for him soon, Looks like there is not much we can do here after all."

Glenda makes to leave, I don't know what came over me, but I signal for her to wait. We can't just leave. There must be something we can do. That, I can do.

"There must be something we can do. What happened originally?" The words spill out of my mouth, hurtful as if they are made of dark iced shards of glass piercing my throat as it is voiced.

Glenda sighs, turns to face me fully, the thin woman goes back and forth wringing the wet cloth she uses on Cents forehead. Her eyes are blank, sad and almost unseeing as she moves around the dull unpainted sparsely furnished room.

"The mob gets him. The sister is arrested, she gets out after a few years but the damage is done, she sets off the pattern of always seeking abusive men."

"Oh no." I breath. The exhale fills the room, and I look around. The woman is crying and asking Cents to quit being feverish as she doesn't know what to do. On closer look, I realise she is probably not even a full grown woman, might be fifteen or less. But hardship I guess, has hardened her features over the years. Her body succumbed to the rigours of being born into hardwork, I can't imagine. She is younger than fifteen but looks twenty three. Her skin burnt to a darker shade of black than Cents, a dull shine to it. I swallow a sob threatening to burst out of my throat.

"You have less than five minutes to do anything. The mob are on their way."

"What do I do?" I ask dumbly. My eyes fixed on the thin girl's shivering shoulders, hunched over the huge dark figure on the ground.

Glenda gives a shrug. I bit my tongue from lashing out at her. She did say she was only going to assist with the time traveling, but let's face it, I can use more help here.

"How about she escapes? At least that is better than watching the mob get him?" Even as I say it, I know it's horrible. Leaving her brother in this state is something no sister would ever do.

"Hm. Well." Glenda says, her beautiful face looks to be thinking hard.

"Forget it, it's wrong. We have to save both of them." I wave a hand to dismiss what I said earlier.

"Would knowing that he beat her within an inch of her life the day before after coming back from killing the man, change your mind?"

"What?" My head whips around to watch the girl again,

clearly this time. She's thin, painfully so and her dirt stained brown dress sits hanging on her slender shoulders like a cloth on a rack, her face though tear stained, has tell tale signs of injuries, I now notice her stride is funny looking, and she grimaces every time she has to bend down.

"It is a messy situation here. He is abusive to her, their relationship is not like the typical brother- sister one you might relate to. They have a rough history, and they are only binded by blood. No formalities. In fact, I think escaping will just be the best solution here. At least given the fact that we arrived late and things are already set in motion, we can only salvage what we can."

It is a lot to take in all at once. Going from being disgusted at myself for suggesting we separate them at such a crucial time, to suddenly advocating for it leaves me almost dizzy. I need to constantly remind myself that this is a different time. Different people. The things these people have had to go through, endure, survive, changes even saints. I can't judge, but it doesn't stop me from feeling nauseous about the whole idea.

"Okay, how do I help her escape? She doesn't look like she can be convinced to run right away." I say, my hands in a tight fist. The air smell charged, and I feel a buzz setting me off from within. I won't call it excitement, but I'm glad the situation can still be managed.

"You have to take control of her mind. I can help with

that. You'll inhabit her body and I'll guard both of you safely out of the area."

"Woah. Take control of her mind? Sounds interesting. I'm set." We hear a commotion from outside, my blood goes cold with pure unadulterated fear. I don't want to witness one of the most horrific actions history has to offer. A white mob attacking a black man. Seeking blood. I can't. I don't want to. The girl hears the noise too and her eyes are bulging like they want to escape their sockets, they mirror the fear in mine.

Glenda must have seen the panic in my eyes, she nods at me, and I walk to her. She grabs my hand, pinning a finger on my pulse, at the contact, I feel like I'm being sucked through a vacuum. Leaving my body, leaving the facts of matter and space and time, convoluting into pure energy, and before I can savor the feeling, the idea, I feel the opposite of being sucked into a void, a letting out, an uncontrollable gushing, like how a river empties into the sea, and I open my eyes to see that I am staring at Cents on the floor up close. Too close, and a wet cloth is in my hands, folding under the pressure I'm putting it under. I look down at the body and realise what had happened.

I'm in the thin girl's body. Her mind is blank except for a steady thumping that echoes raw fear and pain. I look at the dark abyss of the room that's supposed to be her mind and the baldness of it thugs at my heart. I look at Glenda who is staring back at me in this new body, wistfully. She motions for me to follow her, the girl's body is too thin. I'm used to my weight of 70kg, a great weight for a black mother of two, but this girl, she can't be heavier than 40kg, I'm not used to it,

I sway like the very air itself could manoeuvre me, it takes a minute to get the hang of the new body, putting one thin leg after the other, I follow Glenda through a door I hadn't seen in the dark room before. Cents wake up in that moment, he looks at me, the girl, and frowns deeply like he had not just been shivering off a fever seconds ago, his eyes seemed to beckon to her, and I feel the girl within me wither deeply into the dark abyss of her mind with fear and something that tastes like hate. I turn away from him as the noise from the mob outside gets closer.

CHAPTER
Six

The thin girl's name is Nan, and she is actually sixteen years old. She has a black boyfriend whose name is Freeman and they both had a romance going on. Glenda directed us to him at his family's house which is a good sixty miles from the town she lived in with Cents. Safe. Far away from everyone that knows her. Safe from the white mob. Safe from the shadows of Cents.

The closer we got to him, the more I felt her awakening and questioning the reality of her body not being controlled by her. Her fight is weak and sometimes resigned, but it was like each time she realised we are headed to Freeman, the more she wanted to take control of her body again. I hope Glenda has a memory wiping spell, for both of us because this is beyond unbelievable. No one will believe her that she didn't know how she got here, and I'm definitely not going to tell anyone about this mind control, body transfer, time traveling trip. No way.

Finally, she regains control and I'm expelled out of her, almost rudely. The shock of the expulsion shakes my whole core. I'm not used to this type of situation and I didn't know to alert Glenda that the spell was breaking and I needed to be out of her head, so when I find myself in that non-existential space, floating but not really, breathing, but not really, seeing, but not really, untethered and yet hooked to everything that's ever existed, I might have stayed for too long before Glenda pulled me out and into my own inanimate translucent body away from it.

An headache comes on, spreading over my skull like spit fire, licking at every sensitive nerve, it's like being spiked and getting strangely used to the pricking. I watch as Nan is embraced by Freeman who was more scared of being seen, than surprised or excited to see her. I watch her face twist in an inaudible sob, a look of disbelief and shock on her face, then he finally directs her into the small grey painted house, and I lose consciousness then. Satisfied that she is safe. I let go.

I wake up to Glenda's fingers pressing on my pulse. We are back in the green field that stretches till it connects to the light blue horizon. The thought that maybe this place isn't even real, a sort of mid-way spot for time travellers, crosses my mind but is chased off with worry as I remember how Nan's story ended. How she expunged me from her mind and body, if she was better off staying in that small house that is home to a whole family already.

"What happened?" I asked. Glenda looks me in the face as if checking for something, after a moment, she sighs, sits on the soft grass beside me.

"You passed out from the switch. I didn't know the spell broke, and you spent way too much time in the Great-Nothing." She says like she is reciting a chore.

"The great what?" An image of being non-existent and yet being alive flits into my mind and I almost shiver from fright.

"The portal you pass through to both time travel and jump bodies. It is a consciousness not accessible to humans. It is actually less risky because you are invisible and hence close to being inanimate like the rest of us heavenly bodies, but still, it is dangerous to stay in that place too long. Why didn't you let me know you were loosing the grip on Nan's mind?"

"I didn't know for sure, Glenda. I've never been in that type of situation before. It is even crazy to think this is all real."

"Well, you've got a point."

"So. How did that go? Is she going to be okay? Will she remember not being in control of her mind? Have we driven her crazy?" I push a finger against my temple, applying pressure as her face when she was being embraced by Freeman comes to me. She looked bewildered, for lack of a better word.

"Okay, calm down. She won't remember or even have any memory of it. She escaped and made her way to her lover. That's all it was."

"Oh. That's good." Even as I say it, I don't believe it. Because then, we won't have this long chain of trauma and I won't be here in the first place. She escaped going to prison and the unimaginable horrors of it, but she still has the trauma of being raped, being abused by her brother and not truly having anyone to talk to. She is the true root of the pattern. This pattern of bottling up everything. Not seeking help, even when needed because we are scared, terrified of being judged, of our lives being upturned by the confession, of things going awry and having to deal with the thought that if we had just kept our mouths shut, things wouldn't have gone bad. Like Nan did. Like Nan would raise her kids to do. And her kids would raise their kids to do.

I sit up, looking around me, and gazing longingly at the clear skies, inhale the fresh air that seemed to be replenishing my soul, feel every single thing that can be felt. I feel ready, in my bones, but more in my head, ready to do my next time jump and hopefully we are not too late this time around.

"Where in time do we go next?" I say to Glenda with a half grin on my face, she returns the half smile and together, in the bleakness of my ancestors history, we have a full smile.

"You mean, *when* in time do we go next?" She says.

CHAPTER
Seven

LOUISIANA, 1900.

The jump this time does not disorient me as much as the last time, it happened pretty fast and seamlessly, the pause in the Great-Nothing, a blur in time, insubstantial that it does not affect my overall state of mind. It's really amazing how much attitude can alter ones outlook on certain things. I feel slightly shaken up but nothing more.

We are back to the Freeman's family house. The little house is surrounded by a lawn that was neat back in 1870, but now, 30 years later, it looks abandoned. Unattended to. The neat shiny grey paint used on the house is peeling off in large patches. The exterior of the house itself looks like it has seen better days. It's unsettling to witness such a drab decline in the aesthetic of the house. I literally just saw it minutes ago, and now it has gone through 30 years of neglect. I have no sense of actual time, my internal clock is all messed up so I take a while to get accustomed to this new look.

The neighbourhood had seen some advancement, it's like the house and the environment it finds itself in went opposite ways in terms of improvement. The community advanced generally in view of the better state of other freshly painted houses with neat lawns and trimmed flowers on front porches, lively kids with more meat on their bones playing heartily in the warm sun, adults in better clothing with faces that are less gaunt. The church at the far end of the little town, almost on the outskirts has been repainted and had bright hibiscuses and lilies arranged around it, the polished cross at the top glistening against the sun. Everything around the Freeman's house has seen some improvement, yet the house stands in a stark contrast. My heart sinks in a free fall to my uterus. It's really bad if things look this way. What had happened?

"I know this must be hard, but you have to brace yourself. These are crucial times in your family's history and it wasn't pretty." Glenda says, sparing me a glance before looking back at the house, her face doesn't show any emotions but her stance betrays her. She seem weighed down. Like she doesn't want to be here but has no choice. It's the first time I'm seeing a lapse in her stoic demeanour. It scares me a little.

"What happened? Did Nan end up here?" I ask, my voice

takes a while to sound like my own to me. The words float to Glenda like a weird string of depressing music notes.

"Looks like it. Let's go in."

The door slams open, its hinges loose from the force and an aged man with rabid like angry eyes stomps out, I try to escape walking in his direct path, but his footsteps falls into mine before I had the chance and he stomped right through my translucent invisible body. Barely registering the fact, he walks off in an angry blur of curse words and teeth kissing sounds. I not only smell, but also strongly feel the sharp sting of alcohol waft through me. It's nauseating beyond words. Glenda walks through the wall besides the door, looking back at me quizzically, surely wondering why I didn't follow her instead of trying to go in the house through the door like a normal person. Like I wasn't transparent and able to float. I'll need several getting used to, besides I don't even want to be used to being invisible or translucent. That's insane.

The house is dark, even though it's afternoon and bright outside. It's like the light stopped at the door and turned back. I can make out sparse old weather-beaten looking furniture in the room, then in the far end of the living room that tapers off into a rather short hallway of four rooms, two on each side, I spot Nan on a sewing machine. I know it's Nan immediately because I see her fear, familiar and stale, surrounding her like a blanket.

She's still thin, a brown scarf is tied tightly around her head, and her black skin looks worned out, the way black skin tends to look like when it had gone for too long without a moisturiser. I get the same sense of abandonment I got from the house's exterior. She let herself go. It's incredibly sad watching her hunch over the machine, something obsessive about the way her legs press on the pedal, the way her eyes, blank and maybe unseeing tracks the line of cloth she's stitching. I feel a pang of despair. She should be forty six, but she looks entirely way older, too stressed out, too tired, too burdened. I want to sink back on the floor and cry. Cry for her. Cry because it was unfair. So unfair.

"That was Freeman stomping out the door. They got married and inherited the house from his parents after they passed. Freeman's older brother, Henry lives with them. Years of hardwork and poverty has Freeman becoming a drunkard, hence abusive to Nan. He also didn't like that she got raped by a white man before he could have her. Didn't like the baggage she came with. That put a dent on their relationship from the beginning. She also works hard to cater to their family, but she just lost her caretakers job after her client died, in between waiting to get assigned to another client, she takes up sewing. They have three kids together, two girls and one boy. The boy is the oldest and he went North, to New York. The eldest girl is 13 and the youngest is 10. We are here for them. And the positive thing here is that we arrived in time to save the youngest girl from being abused by Henry, who has been abusing the eldest girl since she was also 10."

I press a finger to my temple. I feel the pressure against my skin and it feels good. This situation is uglier and messier than I anticipated.

"Where are the girls?" I ask, my eyes shut tightly, a yearning in my soul lits up slowly. This one hits close to home. I also have two girls and I can't imagine them undergoing what these girls did. Makes me remember the motive behind me accepting to go on this deeply spiritual journey. The reason why I needed this chance to correct things. I simply can't imagine my girls having to deal with something like this. I'm extremely grateful I was granted the opportunity to do this.

"And does Nan know about this?" I shoot a glance at the hunched figure, the sight is sad and stirs a pain deep within my soul. I don't want to think about how hard her life must have been. How hard it will continue to be for the rest of her life. How unfair everything is. How sad it is that this was her life.

"No. The girl didn't tell her. She bottled it up, Henry gets his way with the youngest daughter, successfully traumatizing both links to the present family tree. But I think you can change that, we can save one of them."

"Hell yeah! I will."

We make our way into the girls room, they are both asleep on the only bed in the room. My breath catches at the resemblance the eldest girl has with Lorraine. They have the same exact nose. Broad at the bridge, but patters off at its tip, a kind of upside down button nose. Lorraine was bullied for it in middle school and I remember her being insecure about it for the longest time.

"Okay, this will be easier. Taking over a sleeping mind

makes the spell hold on for longer." Glenda motions for me, I walk over to her, still dazed trying to process what the stunning resemblance might mean. Is she the direct link to me?

Her fingers make contact with my pulse and everything goes dark. I come awake to my body feeling very different. The difference is distinct, the teenage body a foreigness I am unfamiliar with. I look at Glenda, she nods at me. The switch is successful. The girl did not even stir, still deep in her sleep, it's a wonder. And makes my inhabitation less dramatic unlike the one I did with her mother 30 years old, which to me happened a few minutes ago.

"Okay. Go tell Nan about what Henry is doing to her. It's very important she speaks up. That will successful sever the bottling up pattern." Glenda says turning to slip through the wall out of the room. I watch the little sister sleeping peacefully, her long lashes framing a soft innocent pretty face. Something akin to motherhood love stirs in me. I'm grateful to be able to help her avert this curse.

"Betty? You're awake?" Nan blinks at me in her daughter's body, I make a show of rubbing the sleep out of my eyes and doing a stretch. Betty snuggles deeper into her slumber within me. Glenda sits across from us on one of the only two wooden chairs in the living room. She looks to be illuminating the room with her light, but of course it is only visible to me, I doubt Nan notices the change in the room's lighting.

"I have to tell you something, Ma." I don't know why I expected my voice to sound like mine so I put in the effort to sound soft and girlish, what comes out of my mouth is a low bass. Soft, raspy and booms on certain syllables, making her speech heavily accented. Lorraine talks this way. She highlights words in her sentences and it all comes together like she wants to break into a cheerful song but refrains at the last minute. The stunning resemblance is doing my head in.

"What is it? Are you hungry? Where is your sister?"

Nan might be an absent-minded mother, but she tries her best. For the girls. But her best is not close to being enough. In Betty's head, I can see the familiar dark abyss echoing with a potent mix of fear, hate and raw pain. It is profoundly overwhelming how much a child this age can bottle in, seal up in the deep recess of her mind and still manage to lead a normal life that fools her mother to thinking all is well. The adults in her life. I don't dare prod into her mind further, to get the details of the abuse, it would scar me, in addition to my own scar from being abused at thirteen also. Also it might stir her awake and we would start fighting for dominance because this must be her greatest nightmare. Opening up to her mother about being consistently abused by a close family member.

"She's still sleeping. I'm not hungry, Ma."

"You know you have to get as much rest before starting your job in the Collins house. Is your maid uniform clean? You can't resume at a job looking unprofessional. Come sit between my legs so I can clean up your braids."

Nan turns her body away from the machine, she spreads her legs and beckons for Betty. I send a look across to Glenda who makes a signal that I interpret as playing along. I didn't know the girl was going to start working at such an early age, for a job as strenuous as being a maid in a white household. But I understand it might be necessary. The level of poverty in the household is astounding. I didn't grow up wealthy, but things were not this bad. I did summer jobs, still it is nothing compared to being a maid. And I got access to education that further helped me in establishing myself as an entrepreneurial powerhouse. These girls do not look got an education that went beyond the basics.

I settle on the floor in between Nan's legs, her fingers start massaging my scalp, the sensation spread throughout my body like a sweet fire, I relax into the feeling. Glenda moves from behind us, coming to sit in front of me, she makes a gesture of tapping her wrists, I note that it means we can't stay for too long. I take a deep breath, form the words in my gut.

"Uncle Henry touches me." I blurt out. Nan hands pause mid-scratch in the thick hair. The spiritual effects of the words cause a huge stirring within me that unsettles the very fabric of my being. I realise too late that it is Betty awakening. And her will to take control is stronger, like she wants me to eat back the words I had just said.

"Your uncle Henry does what?" Nan voice is shaky. I push myself out of the nook between her legs so I can look at her face. It is a mask of fear, disbelief. She can't even summon anger. I'm truly very sorry to do this to her. But there's no other way.

"He started doing it on my tenth birthday. He comes to the

room when you and Pa are out, and he puts his hands in me. He makes me lick and touch his..."

Nan's shriek force the words to pause in my throat. The sound is guttural and if she wasn't standing in front of me, I would have believed the scream came from a wild animal. She clutches her head in her hands, her tightly wound scarf slips off under the pressure. Her face is hidden from me.

"Henry? Betty. Henry? Betty." She repeats in shock. Her features are marred by pain. It is almost physical, I can almost see her heart breaking. Watch it shatter under the weight of the realisation that she couldn't protect her daughter from the horrible fate she suffered.

"I think he wants to start doing same to my sister, Jane." I apply the final touch as Betty wins the fight over the access to her mental space. It is too much for her, I can understand and it breaks my heart to see her fighting, pushing and pulling me to refrain me from saying more. I can taste her fear, so vivid and wild.

Glenda is there to put me back in my invisible state I've been in since this journey started. But I'm too shaken from moving realities within such a short time. The last thing I see is Nan holding Betty tightly to her chest, tears flowing freely from both of them.

CHAPTER Eight

"You did well." Glenda was saying as I regain consciousness. We are outside the house and I can hear a huge ruckus going on inside. The heavy thump of Freeman's loud baritone voice ripping through the small house, a small crowd of kids is forming at a distance away from the house. My head feels fine. Whatever Glenda does to rehabilitate me, works perfectly well. I may need her for when I return back to my normal life after this surreal experience. To work her magic on the migraine that kicks in after putting in long hours being both a mom and a badass successful entrepreneur.

"What's going on?"

"Freeman is chasing Henry out of the house. It will be a tough battle for every one involved especially Betty, but

I believe we have done our best. Betty opened up. Jane is saved. You have just severed the toxic chain of not being able to speak up when hurt. Well done."

My head wells up in elation, finally this was a situation that was successfully salvaged. Being on time always had its advantages. This is one lesson I'm forever trying to teach May, that girl has zero timeliness in her body. Suddenly I miss my girls and want to wrap up this experience so I could give them a long hug, sniff their hair and share generous kisses.

A smallish man with a foul moustache steps out of the house and his presence draws me back to the current situation, his face is clouded in shame and also equal parts angry. His eyes looks like a wounded feral scavenger animal. I don't need anyone to tell me that this is Henry. I want to spit on the bastard. Anger wells up in me. But I understand we have done enough. I would like to cause him harm, inhabit his rotten head and make him harm himself, but I won't sacrifice my energy on him. He is not worth it. There are other Henrys in our lineage that needs to be dealt with, and in time too. I turn to Glenda.

"Now, where next?"

She gives me a slight smile and I correct myself.

"Oh, I mean, whennext?" I say wringing my hands together, eager to leave this place. Get to the other timelines before it is too late.

"That's better. Come." Glenda reaches for my wrist and

like before, I feel the rush of pressure that being sucked into a vacuum must feel like, a rushed pulling in that leaves me dizzy with momentary confusion and then the opposite, a letting out. A whoosh of air and a splash of wind in my face as I steady my feet to balance on the ground beneath them. It's solid underneath me and I can feel the development in the air before I look around me.

"Your jumping has gotten better." Glenda says, my wrist still in her hand, she looks sideways at me and then let go.

NEW ORLEANS. 1935.

Glenda's face twist in a frown and my heart starts beating fast, her expression can only mean one thing, and it is heartbreaking. We are late. Something has already happened and it might not be salvagable.

The city of New Orleans is very different from what it developed into in my time. The air has that distinct freshness that I've come to identify with a car-less era, but I can sense that that is also changing along with the fashion, with the introduction of automobiles, there are a few on the street, but the majority of the mode of transport is brisk walking to the train station, I can't see it, but I can hear it off in the distance, and the sky is clear. I also note, nostalgically that most of the people walking are blacks.

Their downtrodden shoulders, faces hidden in scarves by the women and the men fast walking like they want to be invisible. This is a very important decade as the great depression started officially now. If things were hard for the elite whites, I wonder how the blacks survived. The financial upheaval will surely see blacks struggling beyond relief. I don't know which of my ancestors we're here for yet, but I know they would be battling with poverty as well. And somehow, I don't want to have to deal with it. It'll make me feel a lot of things, things that have been successfully clouded and forgotten with my success as an entrepreneur. I feel like my success is a payback for all the hardship my ancestors had to go through. Not just me, Lorraine and Charles also. Our relative comfort in life now might be payback for all these.

"Betty has unfortunately gone through what would ultimately define her life for the short rest of it."

Glenda looks at me, we are on a rather busy side walk, and pretty white women in groups of twos and threes are passing by like they are in a public fashion display, in their frock dresses, thigh length socks and heavy looking neck pieces hanging low on their chest. I busy myself with watching them, and noting the sharp contrast with the few black women passing by. How could they not see it? Or even care? Humanity really do test God.

"She got impregnated by her white boss, from that maid job she was to resume thirty years ago, she lost the job, birthed a mixed kid and drowned it at two weeks old. I can't explain her train of thought, the logic behind it, but I am sure it has to do with the time frame and the fact that having a mixed kid is not natural and acceptable. Mixed kids go through hell here."

Glenda says, mistaking my silence for interest in knowing what happened. I kept quiet because I didn't. I feel let down. I was optimistic about how the last episode ended and yet here we are.

"Hm. What about Jane?"

"Oh, she got married. She doesn't have the trauma because she was so young and now the only problem she has is the same as everyone. Financial issues. She's up north too."

That doesn't make me feel better. I stare up at the apartment facing the side walk adjacently, it is a two storey building shaped like an incomplete cube, because it is erected at an intersection between two street. The building is painted a dull yellow, like the colour lost its sunshine and a permanent cloud is over it, the yellow has disintegrated into a dull grey.

"So, how is Betty in general?"

"Not very good. She has a mild case of schizophrenia."

Oh good Lord.

"That's actually very bad." I say wistfully. The enthusiasm sapped off completely.

"There's a sliver of hope though. I think we landed here for a major reason. You see, she continues functioning despite needing clinical help. She meets a bottom barrel no good man at her receptionist job and they birth kids, not even having the decency of getting married first, she passes on untreated anxiety down the line. And other offshoots of her ailment. I'm sure you have an idea what I mean."

I nod, my eyes on the flock of white women that are walking in a vertical line, their dresses are in different colours, but the same style, they smell rich, and I look till they pull into the restaurant opposite the side walk.

"What's the sliver of hope? What can I do for her?" I'm trying to detach from her. So it hurts less. I don't even want to think about the mixed child she killed off in such a brutal method. Why couldn't she just do an abortion? How can any mother birth a kid only to kill it? What was she thinking? Was it a side effect to her mental disorder?

"You can help her seek help. But even that is a bleak option because care for mentally ill people is almost non existent."

"Can't you just heal her?"

"No. It doesn't work that way. Trust me, I wish I could. But it has to be you, doing something to change the pattern."

"I don't want her to end up in an asylum." That's not even a solution I'm willing to look at. As a black woman in the 19th century, ending up in an asylum is the worst fate to have. That will be making her situation worse. Not better, not by a long stretch. She is obviously managing her illness well if she has a job she is able to hold down.

"I agree. That won't help." Glenda says, crosses her arm over her chest, it is something May does in one of her bad moods, the thought shakes me up thoroughly and I start crying at the fact that I miss my girls and doing this for them, no matter how hard, bleak and sad, is going to be for a positive result eventually. Glenda looks at me in surprise, her eyes goes soft and she pats my back. My vision is blurry from the tears, and I can't see the city bustle clearly, just the sounds. The whine of automobiles, the click clack of the white womens shoes, the purr of soft laughter and the general dullness of the people of colour going about like an invisible black mist around the city. I allow myself cry as well as I felt I needed. It is funny, crying in this inanimate body, I don't feel the heaving or even the wetness of my tears, but I do feel my heart breaking.

"We would have to resort to a last option. Not safe or has any success records, but we can try. I will be there to help when needed." Glenda says after a while passes and my sobs subsides.

"I'll do anything. Please Glenda, I can't just leave her like that." I say as everything settles within me, back to order, in retrospect my tears might have been considered dramatic, it's not like I will never see my girls again. It is just that I've never been apart from them for this long. How long is all this really? I have no idea of actual time.

"Come, she just got home."

Glenda goes first and I follow closely behind. She enters the apartment through the front door, and we levitate over the dark staircase, up to the second floor. There is a long hallway that ends at a small opened security office that is unoccupied currently, I see a black woman in a brown frock dress that hugs her slim body in a sexy way, she is slim in the right places and thick in the right places also, I know it is Betty because she has her hair in an updo, I will remember that thick black mane of hair anytime. My hair doesn't come close, but there is something similar with Jules soft curly hair.

Glenda walks through the wall ahead of Betty, I stay watching her jam her keys with an impatience that is also very similar to how Jules get when she is not having her way with something. Her eyes crossed to slit, her lips in a mid pout and a bead of sweat is forming on her brow, her feet is tapping on the floor and she looks about ready to scream if the keys don't work in the next second. Finally, the door clicks open, she sighs and walks into the apartment, turning on the light as she goes. I follow through the door before she closes it back with a thunk.

"You will switch into her head and try getting rid of as much junk as you can within a very short period of time so we don't exacerbate her condition because she is currently active and would definitely feel the switch. She would fight back, but you have to take her through her trauma, of both the consistent abuse from Henry, then the rape affair with her boss, then finally the drowning of the baby. She has to confront those memories. That should do something." Glenda says as soon as I walk into the room.

Betty drops her bag and goes straight to an already opened liquor bottle, she takes a swig directly from the bottle, kicks off her shoes and settle into the armchair that faces her bed in the one room apartment she stays in.

"Okay. Let's do this." I say with false bravado.

"I'll be right here to prevent any disaster." Glenda says softly as she reaches for my wrist. My translucent body disintegrates till I'm a floating blob of energy, and a force pushes me into a dark room that consumes me and chases off the energy that powered the push.

"Anna? Anna?" I open my eyes and Glenda is there, watching me intently. I realise I'm staring back at her from a physical body, a familiar body at that.

I open my mouth to respond but find that I have lost my voice.

"What's this? Again?? I can't deal with this today! I have work tomorrow!" Betty screams at Glenda from inside her head and her voice comes out broken, loud and sob stained. The reaction shakes me to my core. I start panicking.

"Calm down, Anna? Calm down. She believes she is having one of her schizophrenic episodes. It is one of the symptoms. Look inwards and calm her down." Glenda voice cuts through the fog of my blind panic. It makes sense. I look inwards at the snapping Betty, crouched in a corner of the dark room, she looks at me with a mix of disbelief and anger, I raise my hands up in good nature, she hisses at me.

"I'm here to help," I whisper to her, "I promise. Betty. Please."

She cocks her head at me, like she is thinking about it. Like she is no longer wondering why I'm here or what in hell's name was going on, she is looking at me in a way that shows she needs whatever help I might be offering.

"Why did you do it, Betty?" Not a good first question, but Glenda did mention we don't have much time. I don't want to be stuck here.

She sinks into her corner, half of her body hidden away, I look closely to see her shoulders shaking uncontrollably, her lips are quavering and her eyes are wild, unseeing. I feel a pang of pain. Her physical body drops the alcohol bottle, and I flinch away from the broken bottle.

"It was for the best. I swear. It was for the best. She was sickly and this world did not deserve her. I'm so sorry but I don't regret doing it. What would I have done with a sickly fatherless mixed child? She would have had a tough time in this wretched world." She howls. Her hands clutching at her hair desperately. Her wild eyes look to be settling down.

"Okay, that is okay, I understand. She is an angel, your personal angel." I say soothingly.

"She is? She is, right?" Betty looks up to me, her face tear streaked, in that moment an image of Nan crosses my mind, they both look familiar in their misery.

"Yes, she is. You have to forgive yourself and move on Betty."

"Right? I should." She says, her constant need for affirmation makes her seem child-like. Soft, innocent and an emotional mess.

"Yes." I walk deeper into the dark room, beside her, she is holding tightly to a cloth, I pry it out of her hands, it is a baby cloth. She looks at me in shock, but I nod and give her a smile, she lets go completely and heaves a sigh of relief. I fold the cloth neatly, tucking it away.

"You're not crazy and you'll be just fine, Betty. Without this. All of this. You don't need them anymore." I say gesturing to the pile of baby things clattering the room. Even though it is dark, I can see them clearly. These are her mental baggages.

"I don't, right?" She looks up at me, her face a picture depicting a strong need for validation. I nod, with a smile on my face.

"Yes, you don't."

"Thank you." She says springing up to her feet, she starts plowing through the packages, kicking and throwing them as far as she could. The dark room is expanding to accommodate the onslaught. I join her.

"You have to get out, now." Glenda authoritative voice flits into the barrage.

"Who are you, anyways?" Betty says as I start pulling back from her, the force strong and persistent.

I smile a sad smile, "a friend. Nice to be of help, I wish you a good life Betty."

The last thing I remember is Betty returning my smile, a promise as she goes back to discarding the packages.

CHAPTER
Nine

NEW ORLEANS, 1970.

Glenda didn't need to tell me who we were coming to meet this time around, I knew. Call it intuition or whatever, but I have been able to notice a pattern in the time jumping. The years we visit and the women we meet. Helping Betty twice in different times made me realise she was my direct grandmother. I now recall that in my reality, stories of a member of the family who got pregnant but didn't produce a child after the pregnancy, was whispered and talked about in hushed tones, on very rare occasions. Betty is still alive in 1970, but she's old and retired having managed to make something positive out of her life. Got married to the average black man, who wasn't abusive, a very important factor, went on to birth five black kids, the last of which was my mom, Nina.

I didn't have the typical mother daughter relationship with my mom growing up, we were not close, neither were we distant. We were at an in between that I can't even describe. If anyone asked me to describe my mother in a word, I would say, indifferent. But not in the harmful sort of way, she was warm to us at the appropriate times, when we got scratches from playing roughly, when we needed food, when we got sick, in situations where she was needed, she provided the necessary comfort, but there was always an aloofness to her. Always a perfunctory application to the way she tended to us, I got the idea that she was not present most times, not because she didn't care, but she couldn't help it.

"Well, you know who we are here for, I'm glad we got here before you were born. Else, we'd have serious complications if both energies collided." Glenda is saying as I am once again lost, taking in the 70s. The turn of a new decade. There's that crispness in the air, swollen to bursting with good cheer and general excitement. New decades are always special, they feel like a new leaf. A second chance. A new beginning. That is what my mom always said, anyways.

"Nina did not speak up about her experience with her boyfriend's older brother who tried to rape her but didn't succeed due to a distraction and promised her a second opportunity to get at it. I know Jude had his way with you, I'm terribly sorry." Glenda says.

there was an actual rule demarcating the expansive park, or maybe it just came to be, however that could happen. I just notice that the whites are not mixing with the blacks. It is distinctly separate. A sight for sore eyes. Racism like this is not in my normal timeline, it is more subtle, but there nonetheless. Seeing all I've seen so far, I am wryly grateful for how far we have come as a people, against all odds. We are still here, living with kindness and greatness in our hearts despite the fact that as a people we have been dealt the worst hand in all of humankind history.

I see my dad before I see my mom and how young they look takes me aback. My dad has a head full of hair, a moustache that's neatly primed, and he has on a loose t-shirt and wide legged pants. His broad shoulders are free, his waist tiny and his muscly legs are long. It is such a sharp contrast to what he is now, in my timeline. Such a sharp sharp contrast, I don't think he remembers who this man is. Who he had been. I don't think he remembers laughing with this ease. Head thrown back and his laugh bubbling from his stomach.

As for my mom, I find it hard to accept what I'm seeing as reality. As the last kid, they had me after a whole twelve years of being together. Twelve years later and capitalism had succeeded in stealing this soul they had. This freeness. This glibness. This youthfulness. I didn't have old parents per say, but I never knew my dad to be this handsome with less stress lines on his face. Nor did I have a mom who looked as carefree as she did here, twelve years ago. How long is twelve years really? For such a drastic change.

"Okay, same drill. I'll do the spell, you get in and get out, quick. This is a public place and she is in high spirits. You just have to come out in the right moment and say what she is contemplating to say, then I'll pull you out. Your real timeline needs you." Glenda finishes with a wink. I don't know what she means by it, but I offer her my wrist nonetheless. Even though I am sceptical, and generally reluctant to do it, I know it is important. The last link to me. For my girls, this is important. I don't know if my life will be different if Jude didn't rape me at thirteen, because frankly, I believe I did a good job of blocking away the memory and when he died, I took it as my reparation. But still, I understand these things don't really go away. They manifests and transcribe into a new DNA in our offsprings. I know this now.

"Nina? Nina, you said you wanted to talk about something. What's it that is bothering you?" My dad holds my hands, staring lovingly into my eyes. I almost cry at the affection. I didn't get an affectionate dad also. I come to terms with the fact that the switch this time was even more seamless. Glenda is hovering above dad's head and watching me inside mom intently.

I feel her stir, contemplate one last time and decides it wasn't worth it to ruin the beautiful moment they were having, I watch her search for something else to talk about instead, I watch her eyes lit up, the way I never got to see all through her lifetime with me, when an idea appeared to her. And still I watch when her eyes catch mine, she recoils away from me, fear thumping like a third heartbeat in the closed off room that was her mind.

I shake my head at her, she stares in shock, blinking like a child. I give her a half smile meant to reassure her.

"Jude tried to rape me two weeks ago and he promised to have his way next time." I say as she watches me, first I saw confusion, then anger and finally fear. She didn't like that I told dad. Now I have the word that better describes her, it is selfish. It makes better sense this way.

"What?" Dad's loud voice bellows and the reverberation can be heard from a distance. I watch as some white moms pull their kids closer to them.

"Tim, I'm sorry, I didn't mean to say that. Oh my god, I don't know what I was thinking." Mom is back in control of herself, she tries frantically to backtrack, casting angry looks at me. I drag her away from the drivers seat, not a physical thing, more a mental strength than anything physical, we are beyond the physical realm in here.

"What exactly are you saying, Nina?" Dad grabs my hands again, shaking me to repeat myself.

"Jude tried to rape me two weeks ago. Remember when we were at your place watching cable and you went to get drinks in the downstairs store? He groped me and was really rough on me. I was scared and then you got back earlier than expected and he backed off, promising me a second encounter. I was terrified, I didn't know what to do or say. I've been meaning to tell you, but it is hard."

Mom yanks me off and takes control again, her frantic eyes

betraying her confusion as to how to to handle the situation. I decide I had done enough when dad springs up from his seating position and starts stomping off the park. Mom tries to follow him but she can't catch up with his strides, her face is tear streaked and she looks mad. But confused also, like being shown a video of you sleep walking.

Glenda pulls me out and I'm able to watch her from outside of her head, pack up the picnic and follow him out of the park.

CHAPTER
Ten

"So, this is it." Glenda says giving me her first wide smile. Her face lits up like a million sunsets. I pause to watch her. Try to commit her face to memory, but I know it is a futile try, she would wipe every trace of herself and this experience from my memory.

"Yeah, this is it. I'm super grateful I was granted this opportunity. It has been surreal. I don't have the words." I say, inhale, hold it, to get in all this clean air, all this life giving lushness around me, then I exhale, slowly, ravishing the release.

"I guess you already know that you'll not remember all of this. When you get back to your timeline, it will be one free of generational traumas and memories of abuse. Your girls are getting a clean slate." Glenda says.

I stare at the horizon, it really does end where the grasses touch it. There is no way it doesn't. The expansive green field we're in smells like a thousand blooming lilies. It is intoxicating. I might miss it. But then, I know I won't because I won't remember.

"Yeah, it's for the best. I know." I say with a sigh.

"But, give me a minute before you chase me off to my timeline." I say dramatically. Glenda laughs airily. I like the sound of it. Life is really full of mysteries, we just live each day as they come without paying attention to the things that goes on in the spiritual realm. I can't believe I now have experienced the spiritual. But it is a bittersweet feeling because I can't take the memories to my reality. Once I cross back, everything would be erased. But I think I would take solace in having a clean slate for my girls. A different improved mental space for myself, without the rape from Jude ever happening. I don't mind not remembering this surrealness if it comes with my mental health being improved and my girls not having to deal with the generational trauma plaguing my life. The chain severed and staying severed forever.

I look at Glenda who is staring off into the horizon, her face a picture of contentment and graceful joy, I can't believe a being like her exists. Even though I believe in the spiritual, supernatural forces, having a physical manifestation of it in front of me is too good to be real. I'm grateful for her help throughout this journey. I'm so thankful, it fills up my insides. She turns to look at me, my face conjures up a smile and she returns it. The brilliance of her smile almost blinding me.

"I'm ready." I say.

"Well done, Anna. Well-done. Your long line of ancestors thanks you."

I present my wrist to her, but she shakes her head and reaches for my forehead. She presses one light finger to the space between my brows and I feel a gathering of energies from the pit of my stomach, it bubbles upwards and threatens to spill out of my mouth, I clamp it shut, the force builds up and I shut my eyes too.

"You did well, Anna. You did well, Anna. You did well, Anna." The words reverberate around my skull as I open my eyes slowly, my eyelids feel strangely heavy, and my tongue is sour with a medicinal taste in my mouth. I see the clock first, 7:00am. Then the sky blue curtains and the bright white painted room. Then it comes rushing back to me. The car accident. That is where my memories end. I have this feeling that I'm forgetting something important, it is just at the tip of my brain, but it refuses to come out fully. I let it go.

"Moommmmy." It is Jules and her whiny voice crashes into my head as her small body leaps into mine on the bed.

"Now don't jump on her like that, baby girl." I hear Lorraine's rapsy voice as she comes into focus. May is behind her, her eyes bright and wide, a sign that she is been crying. I feel a lump in my throat. Jules is showering my face with kisses, her hair tangling with mine. I forget about any discomfort my body might be in, I beckon to May, she comes to me slowly, dragging her feet, when she finally reaches me, she lets out a sob and hugs my neck tightly, sniffling and crying. I rein in my tears. I don't even know the severity of the accident yet, I can only hope it is not bad.

"How long have I been here?" I ask Lorraine who is pulling Jules off the bed and patting May's back to soothe her.

"What do you mean, how long? The accident was yesterday night. You don't remember anything? They gave you painkillers that made you drowsy and you slept like a log. We were here till midnight, left to go get some sleep and here we are."

Oh. Why did I feel like it's been longer than that? It makes sense that I've only been here a night.

"Ah, the crew is back." A soft voice says from the door, he walks into the room, a doctor with a kind face and a gleaming bald head. He glances at Jules in Lorraine's arm and gives her a warm smile.

"Mrs. Hudson, I am Dr. Jordan and I'm here with good news seeing as you woke up already. We did worry why you you didn't wake up all through the night, had some brain scans done and everything looks good. We can just chalk up your unconsciousness to the painkillers. Anyways, you came in with a dislocated shoulder, we popped that back in, monitored your vitals, you're all good. We can discharge you tonight." He says in one long breath. A nurse calls for his attention from the door, he gives me a gentle smile and rushes back out.

"Well, that went well." Lorraine says.

"What happened to my car?"

"It is going to need at least two mechanic visits and it'll be good as new. Anna, we are lucky the car didn't topple over the levee. Really lucky."

A shiver passes through me at the thought, how close I was to disaster. I feel reawakened. Like something clicked differently. An attachment of spiritual grace. But most of all, I feel grateful. Immensely so. To have another shot at my life, my daughters and the world, a different black woman.

Made in the USA
Columbia, SC
27 July 2024